# WHEN
## *Santa Claus*
# PRAYED

*Always look to the*
*"Brightest Star."*
*Gary Henry*
*2013*

BY GARY HENRY

ILLUSTRATED BY DEANNA HENRY

*Deanna Henry*

xulon
PRESS

*When Santa Claus Prayed*
by Gary Henry
Illustrated by Deanna Henry

Printed in the United States of America

ISBN 9781628396317

Unless otherwise indicated, Bible quotations are taken from The King James Version of the Bible.

www.xulonpress.com

# INTRODUCTION

$\mathcal{Y}$ou may wonder if this is a true story. It is fiction, but it easily could have happened to me as a child. My parents had a selfless devotion to our family, an unbending Christian faith, and a great love of Christmas. I will forever treasure the memories of our family Christmases, which included the childhood enchantment of Santa Claus, but genuinely centered on the birth of Jesus. This story is a tribute to my mom and dad and the role models they were for my brother, two sisters, and me.

As this story took shape in my mind, I found myself wishing I would have thought

GREETINGS
from our house
to your house

Christmas 1957
The Dick Henry's

of it when my three children were young. It has always been a challenge for parents to find an appropriate balance between Santa Claus and the birth of the Christ Child at Christmas. My prayer is that this story will help make it easier for parents and their children to enjoy the endearing childhood stories and traditions of Saint Nicholas while truly and joyously celebrating the birth of our Savior, taking part in the types of giving and receiving our Father intends for all of us.

With all my love and thanks to my wife, Darla

For Neil, Deanna, and Jenna, and their families

Especially for our grandchildren, Kiyah, Asher, Avelyn, …

*ome Christmas memories seem to be more special than others. Maybe an unexpected December storm dumped a foot of snow on Christmas Eve, or we made a trip to visit far away family. Perhaps, it was an amazing present that we received, or a fully-decorated tree, toppled by our new puppy. There is one very memorable Christmas that will be forever etched in the minds of my sister and me for a very different reason.*

For three years my little sister and I had been doing our best to convince Mom and Dad to display our big, plastic, light-up Santa Claus in its rightful place, the middle of the front yard, not around the side of the house where it was barely noticeable. Each year they insisted our Nativity scene, with the wise men and shepherds and all, be placed in front. They said the Nativity was the most important part of Christmas, not Santa Claus.

Well, things turned into a bit of a battle when I was eight and a half. It was three weeks before Christmas. We all worked together hauling the outside decorations down from the garage, including our Nativity set, which we carefully unwrapped from its protective blankets. As usual, we proceeded to set up the Nativity where everyone who was driving by would see. We positioned Mary and Joseph perfectly, and as Dad was carefully arranging the straw in the manger I tried not to complain, but I just couldn't hold back any longer.

"Dad," I declared, "Santa has got to be in the middle of the front yard this year, not the manger scene!" I glanced at Sis for encouragement. Her smile told me she approved. Appearing a bit perturbed, Dad calmly gave his usual speech about how Santa Claus is very important, but the birth of Jesus is the most important reason for celebrating Christmas.

I guess I'd finally had all I could take, so I spoke my piece, rather unpeacefully. "Dad, you're wrong about Santa Claus! I can write letters to Santa. I can sit on his lap and tell him everything I want for Christmas. He is the one who brings presents to us! In case you haven't noticed, he's everywhere! He's on TV and in the stores and magazines..."

It was very evident my dad's patience was wearing thin, but despite all of the warning signs, my mouth was no longer obeying my brain. I really poured it on, growing louder and much more determined. "I can't sit on the Baby Jesus's lap, or even see Him! I can't send letters to Jesus! He doesn't bring me anything for Christmas, and how many TV shows are made about Him?! Obviously, Santa Claus is the *star* of Christmas, so obviously he should be in the middle of our front yard!"

One glance at my dad told me I had reason to be worried. His eyes were squinted and his brow deeply furrowed. His face and neck were suddenly as red as Santa's suit, and with lips drawn thin, he looked as if he was about to explode. I knew I had gone way too far this time. Sis was slowly backing toward my mom. Mom just stood there looking at me. She appeared to be in shock, but thankfully recovered quickly enough to defuse the bomb. She laid a soft hand on my dad's shoulder and calmly said, "Remember, Honey, he's just a little boy." That is the only time I can remember when I didn't mind her calling me a little boy. I feel certain she rescued me from a very early bedtime, with no supper.

Dad took a big, deep breath. The redness began to fade from his face as he patiently explained to me, yet again, why Christmas is not all about Santa Claus. He reminded me that I could talk to Jesus, not just at Christmas, but all year long, and any time of the day or night. He gave me the entire speech about how Jesus is God's Son, born to be our Savior, and that He even gave His life for us. I looked to my sister for help. I knew she was still on my side, but since she always enjoyed hearing me get a good lecture, she stood back and remained silent. I don't think I even listened to the rest of the speech. As you would expect, I lost my case again. My dad, the judge, made his decision, and it was final! Once again, Santa Claus would take a back seat to the Baby Jesus... at least for now.

For the next three weeks we went through our usual preparations for Christmas: shopping, baking cookies, attending school and church programs, taking family pictures, sending greeting cards, and enjoying TV specials. Finally, the time arrived for one of my favorite traditions. Each year, two days before Christmas, my sister and I went shopping with Dad just to buy gifts for Mom. We would always eat at our favorite pizza

place, drop our family's collection of coins in the Salvation Army kettle, and head into the mall.

That night we paused outside the entrance to admire the mall's beautiful Nativity scene. It was perfectly placed at the end of a walkway, surrounded by evergreen trees that sparkled with snow and twinkling lights. Then we proceeded inside to meet with Santa one last time before the big day. After reminding my Christmas hero of the top priorities on my list and my superbly good behavior, we did our best to choose some special gifts for Mom. I don't remember exactly what we picked out for her that year, but I feel certain there was an amazing new kitchen gadget, a pink or blue sweater, a pair of frilly pajamas, a dazzling piece of cheap jewelry, and a bottle of smelly stuff my dad thought was *heavenly*. Finally, we stopped and had the ladies at the Gift Wrapping Center conceal Mom's presents in pretty paper and ribbon. Dad was a sloppy gift wrapper, and he said Mom would snoop if we just took them home in bags.

It was getting late as we prepared to head home. Some shop owners had turned off some lights in hopes of getting home a bit early. A few stores were putting up "Last Minute Sale" posters, and Santa's big, cushy chair sat empty except for a sign reporting, "GONE TO THE NORTH POLE – BE GOOD!!"

As we were leaving the mall, something happened that would change Christmas forever for me. On our way to the parking lot we stopped to look at all of the lights and decorations one last time. When I glanced through the trees toward the Nativity I noticed something unusual. A walk down the pathway revealed Santa Claus, standing in the middle of the scene, among all of the shepherds and sheep. His head was bent toward the manger. He held his hat in his hands, which were folded over his beard. His eyes were closed. I edged closer to him and quietly asked, "Santa, are you okay?"

He opened his eyes, turned, and peered down at me over the top of his glasses. With a kind smile, Santa softly replied, "Of course, Sammy, I'm fine."

"Well… what are you doing?" I wondered aloud.

"Why, I'm praying, Sammy."

"Praying? Why would you be praying? You're Santa Claus!"

"Don't you pray?" he asked.

"Sure I do, but I'm not Santa Claus. Why would Santa Claus pray?"

Santa thought for a moment before answering. "Well Sammy, I am praying because I am very thankful. I have millions of children all over the world who love me. I am blessed to be able to give gifts to them, especially those who really need them. I am also praying that all of those boys and girls and their families might have a wonderful Christmas, not just because of the presents, food, and family get-togethers, but because of the birth of Jesus, our Savior. He is the reason we need to celebrate. And of course, I am praying for the families that don't even know about Him." Then Santa nodded toward the manger and said, "You need to always remember, Sammy, I am not the brightest star of Christmas. He is."

Wow! Talk about having the rug pulled out from under me! I was caught completely off guard. I was dumbfounded. I just stood there beside Santa for a couple of minutes, pondering it all. When I looked up, his eyes were closed again. I walked slowly back to Dad and Sis. As I crawled into the car, Dad looked at me and asked if I was okay. "Yeah," I answered, "I'm fine. But there is something I need to do when we get home."

Dad didn't say another word. It was a quiet ride home. When we got out of the car I told him I would come into the house in just a minute. He went in, but my sister stood on the driveway and watched as I walked around the side of the house. Our plastic, light-up Santa was pretty heavy, but I managed to wrestle him around the house and across the front yard. I dragged him into the middle of the Nativity and stood him right in front of the manger with his back turned toward the road. I noticed the curtains were pulled back, and my parents were peeking out of the window. I figured I would be in big trouble, but I didn't care.

Sis and I took off our coats and shoes, then nervously walked into the living room. Mom and Dad were still standing by the window, staring at me. Dad was speechless. He appeared calm, but puzzled. My sister looked as if she was actually afraid for me this time. Finally, Mom broke the silence. With a very concerned look she asked, "Sammy, why in the world did you just move Santa Claus into the middle of the manger scene?"

Fighting back tears, I swallowed hard and simply answered, "Because tonight… I saw Santa Claus pray." Then I quickly said, "Goodnight," and ran to my room.

When I woke up the next morning it was Christmas Eve. The first thing I did was hurry to my bedroom window. I'll never forget wiping the cold fog from the window with my pajama sleeve and gazing out at the wintery morning. I couldn't believe my eyes! There was Santa, still standing in front of the manger! I ran to the front door and out into the snow, wearing my robe and slippers. I had to be sure it was true. Mom and Dad followed me, with my sleepy-eyed sister trailing behind. They hugged me and said Santa could stay where he was until it was time to take down all of the Christmas decorations! For the next few weeks, when anyone asked them why our Santa was standing in the middle of the Nativity, they just smiled and said, "Because Sammy saw Santa Claus pray."

*I'm all grown up now. Thirty years have passed since that Christmas. I have a home and children of my own. Every year we work together, carefully arranging a Nativity scene in the middle of our front yard. Every year we proudly place our big, plastic, light-up Santa Claus right in front of the manger, among all of the shepherds and sheep. And every year my kids ask me to tell them the story about the Christmas when I saw Santa Claus pray. Yes, even Santa knows that he is not the brightest star of Christmas. In the manger lies the "brightest star" of Christmas.*

"When they saw the star, they rejoiced with exceeding great joy." (Matthew 2:10)

# The Brightest Star of Christmas

When Santa Claus Prayed

Gary Henry and Brian Maguire

# ACKNOWLEDGEMENTS

Special thanks to
Ben Johnson and his dad, Brian,
for being models for Sammy and his dad.

To my Daughter, Deanna, for dedicating her summer to paint
the beautiful illustrations for this book.

To Brian Maguire for his friendship and his support of this entire project.

Most of all, thanks to God for giving us this story.

# ABOUT THE ILLUSTRATOR

eanna Henry, the author's daughter, lives near Pittsburgh, Pennsylvania. She is an elementary art teacher and loves encouraging the imaginations of her students. When not teaching, she enjoys jogging, swimming, reading, and spending time with family and friends.

# ABOUT THE AUTHOR

Gary Henry and his wife, Darla, reside near Rimersburg, Pennsylvania. Gary recently retired after 35 years of teaching at Keystone Elementary School in Knox, Pennsylvania. Throughout his career, he and several of his friends have enjoyed enriching the lives of children and adults, through storytelling and song, at various school, community, and church functions. He also has a great love of the outdoors, especially the challenge and camaraderie of archery and flintlock hunting. He is excited about having more time to devote to these pastimes, his family (especially the grandchildren), and serving God wherever He leads.

CPSIA information can be obtained at www.ICGtesting.com
Printed in the USA
BVOW10s0624051013

332989BV00002B/2/P